fenway
AND THE
FRISBEE TRICK

SNIFF OUT ALL THE

MAKE WAY FOR FENWAY!

CHAPTER BOOKS!

Fenway and the Bone Thieves

Fenway and the Frisbee Trick

DIG UP THESE MIDDLE GRADE BOOKS ABOUT FENWAY, TOO!

Fenway and Hattie

Fenway and Hattie and the Evil Bunny Gang

Fenway and Hattie Up to New Tricks

Fenway and Hattie in the Wild

MAKE WAY FOR

FENWAY

fenway

AND THE
FRISBEE TRICK

VICTORIA J. COE

illustrated by
JOANNE LEW-VRIETHOFF

putnam

G. P. PUTNAM'S SONS

G. P. PUTNAM'S SONS
An imprint of Penguin Random House LLC, New York

First published in the United States of America by G. P. Putnam's Sons,
an imprint of Penguin Random House LLC, 2022

Text copyright © 2022 by Victoria J. Coe
Illustrations copyright © 2022 by Joanne Lew-Vriethoff

Visit us online at penguinrandomhouse.com

Library of Congress Cataloging-in-Publication Data is available.

Printed in the United States of America

ISBN 9780593406946 (hardcover)
1 3 5 7 9 10 8 6 4 2

ISBN 9780593406953 (paperback)
1 3 5 7 9 10 8 6 4 2

LSCC

Design by Marikka Tamura
Text set in Bodoni Six ITC Std

To Teddy Graham,

who showed us the trick.

—V.J.C.

To all the stray dogs in the world,

I hope you will one day find shelter and

love, because you deserve it. —J.L.V.

CONTENTS

1

THE BIG PARK

Romping in the Dog Park behind our house is pretty awesome. But riding in the car with Hattie and Fetch Man is even better, because we're going to the Big Park.

The Big Park has picnic tables. The Big Park has a garbage can. But best of all, the Big Park has a huge grassy space to run and play in.

I love everything about the Big Park—except the squirrels. Squirrels are sneaky.

As soon as our car stops in the crunchy gravel, me and Hattie

tumble out. Hattie loves going to the Big Park as much as I do. Fetch Man can hardly keep up with us.

While we stop to water a small tree (me, not them), I glance around. It looks like we have the whole park to ourselves. The squirrels know better than to show their beady little faces when I'm around.

Hattie unclips my leash, and Fetch Man grabs a stick.

"Ready, Fenway?" he says.

My tail goes nuts, and I rush past the garbage can. "I'm so ready! I'm so ready!" I bark.

I watch Fetch Man's arm whip back, then—FWOOSH! The stick flies through the air.

I sprint after it. "I got it! I got it!" I bark. That stick is mine! TWAAP! It plops down, and I pounce. CHOMP!

I prance back to Hattie, my tail high and proud.

"Good boy, Fenway!" she sings. She pats my head, like she thinks I won't notice Fetch Man's hand reaching for the stick.

I clench my teeth.

"Gimme that stick. Gimme that stick." Fetch Man growls, wearing a wide smile.

After a few pulls and tugs, I let Fetch Man win. That's part of the game.

Fetch Man throws the stick again and again. Each time, I race after it and give it a chomp when it lands. I bring it back to Hattie for a "good boy" and some head pats. Then I let Fetch Man win at tug-of-war.

Fetch is the Best Game Ever!

I've just started racing the stick back to Hattie again when I notice something. A huge Rottweiler trots into the park. A tall human wearing a cap jogs behind her. I've never seen them before.

Hattie rubs my head. "Good boy," she says.

Fetch Man goes for the stick. "Gimme!"

While I'm tugging, I watch a Frisbee whiz through the air. The Rottweiler leaps up, her body twisting, and—wowee!—she snatches it in midair! What an amazing trick!

Fetch Man pulls the stick from my mouth and hurls it.

As I race after the stick, the Frisbee whizzes by a second time. It goes higher and higher. The Rottweiler springs up, flips head over tail, and—whoopee!—snatches it in midair again!

It takes a moment or two before I remember my own stick, lying in the grass.

2

CARMEN

Hattie claps. "WOW!" she cries.

"Cool!" Fetch Man shouts.

They sound impressed. I know how they feel. Those Frisbee tricks are awesome!

The Rottweiler trots through the grass. She holds her tail high.

When she reaches her tall

human, she drops the Frisbee at his feet. He rubs her all over. "Attagirl, Carmen!" he says, laughing.

"Thanks, Felipe!" she barks. "Let's do it again!"

He seems to understand. The moment Felipe reaches for the Frisbee, Carmen springs up like the grass is on fire. She takes off.

"Hey, I want to do awesome tricks, too!" I yell, romping after her.

She doesn't break a stride. "If you can reach the Frisbee first!" she calls.

WHIZZZZZ!

The Frisbee sails high overhead.

Carmen is already past the picnic tables. She's in the middle of the Big Park.

"No fair!" I call. "You had a head start!" I chase her as fast as I can. But she's a lot faster. She pulls farther ahead with every step.

Suddenly, Carmen turns and looks up. The Frisbee is almost directly above her. How did she even know that?

I'm so far back, I don't even stand a chance. All I can do is watch.

Carmen leaps up. She spins completely around. And—CHOMP— she nabs the Frisbee in midair. Again.

I hear Hattie and Fetch Man clapping.

Carmen gallops past me, the Frisbee firmly in her jaws. I follow her back to Felipe. "That was amazing!" I tell her.

She drops the Frisbee at her tall human's feet, and he rubs her all over. "Attagirl! Attagirl!" he cries.

Hattie and Fetch Man rush over. "Woot!" they say.

Carmen drops into the grass for a belly rub. "Way to go, Carmen!" Felipe says.

Everybody sounds impressed. Carmen is on her back, her legs sprawled out and kicking with happiness. She's clearly enjoying all the attention.

This is totally unfair. There's no way I can beat her to the Frisbee. But then I get another idea. While everybody is praising Carmen, I rush across the park to snatch my stick.

I come back and leave it at Hattie's feet. "Throw it again!" I bark, pawing her leg. "I bet I can do tricks like Carmen, too!"

"Oh, Fenway," she says. She does not sound interested, but she takes the stick anyway.

I race out into the grass. "I'm ready! I'm so ready!" I bark.

Hattie's arm goes back. She hurls the stick.

FWOOSH! It flies through the air. I charge after it. When I get past the picnic tables, I slow down. I turn. I leap. I twist. I'm going to nab it in midair!

And then—TWAAP!

I hear the stick land in the grass behind me.

I whip around and stare. Carmen made it look so easy. What went wrong?

Suddenly, I realize the problem. Carmen has a Frisbee. And I don't.

3

THE PLASTIC LID

On the ride home, I know what to do—convince Hattie that I need a Frisbee.

If I had my own Frisbee, I wouldn't have to beat out Carmen to get it first. Then I could leap up and snatch it in midair just like she does. Everyone would clap and cheer for my amazing tricks. All I

have to do is get Hattie to understand how important it is.

I follow her into the Eating Place.
There must be a way to convince
her.

Then she opens a low cabinet
and I see exactly what I need—
a plastic lid! It's shaped just like
a Frisbee!

As Hattie pulls out a bowl, I
poke my snout into the cabinet.
It smells horrible, like
clean dishes. Before
she can shoo me
out—CHOMP—
I grab the
plastic lid.

"Fenway!" she scolds.

I race around the Eating Place, Hattie hot on my tail. It's working!

I lift my head. I shake the plastic lid from side to side like a toy. It's not as big as a Frisbee, but Hattie is smart. She'll get it.

But she doesn't. She keeps darting in front of me, waving her arms. "Fenway, stop!" she cries.

I sprint in the other direction. Why isn't this working?

"Gimme!" Hattie shouts.

And that's when I realize I'm doing it wrong. I spin around and— **PLOP!**—I drop the plastic lid at Hattie's feet.

I gaze up at her. "Toss it!" I bark. "Please?"

For a moment, I think she's got it. Her frown turns into a smile. Then a laugh. She stoops down and picks up the plastic lid.

"I'm ready!" I bark, leaping and spinning. "I'm so ready!"

But instead of throwing it, she puts it in the sink.

I rush up and paw her legs. "You were supposed to toss it!" I bark.

Hattie leans over and pats my head. "Aw, Fenway," she coos. Like everything is suddenly okay.

But it's not.

Later, I'm in the Dog Park behind our house. I finish chasing a squirrel up the giant tree when I hear dog tags jingling. It's my friends Goldie and Patches next door!

I trot over to the fence. "'Sup, ladies?" I say.

I peer through the slats as they lumber toward me.

After exchanging sniffs, I sink down in the grass. I tell them about Carmen and how everybody went nuts over her awesome tricks.

"I want to do tricks like that," I say. "I need my own Frisbee."

"But you don't need a Frisbee to do tricks, Fenway," says Patches. "You already do awesome things."

"Yeah," Goldie says. "You're a dog of many talents."

I look up. "You weren't there. Carmen was amazing. Everybody was clapping and cheering."

"You're amazing in your own way," Patches says.

Goldie scratches behind her ear. "You're full of excitement."

"And energy," Patches adds.

"Any dog can be excited. Any dog

can have energy," I grumble. "I want to do tricks."

I cover my snout with my paws. Now my best friends don't get it, either.

4

THE BIG BROWN TRUCK

A few days later, I'm dozing on the rug in the Lounging Place. I dream about Frisbees.

> *A bright new Frisbee*
> *flies over my head.*
> *I'm looking up . . . I'm*
> *chasing it . . . and—*
> *poof! Hey, it's gone!*
>
> *Another Frisbee sails*

through the air. I'm running after it . . . I'm leaping up . . . and—poof! That one's gone, too!

Oh, but here's another Frisbee! I'm going to get it! Nothing can stop me! I hear it rattling. I hear it roaring . . .

My eyes pop open. And my ears perk up.

A loud rattling and roaring sound is coming through the window. I spring onto the couch. "Danger!" I bark.

Hattie doesn't look up from her book.

I know who it is even before it pulls into view—the Big Brown Truck! It doesn't belong here. So why is it stopping in front of our driveway?

"Warning!" I bark, baring my teeth. "A Jack Russell Terrier is on patrol!"

The truck stays put, but a tall human climbs out. He's carrying a box.

He's walking toward our house. Like he has permission to come right to the door.

I zigzag across the top of the couch. "Hold on there, buddy!" I bark. "I won't let you in without a fight."

DING-DONG!

As soon as the sound chimes, Hattie springs out of her seat. She rushes to the door, and I'm right on her heels. "You can't be thinking of letting this guy in?" I bark.

When Hattie opens the door, I'm ready for trouble. But the tall human is already halfway down the driveway. He's headed back to the Big Brown Truck. And the box he was carrying is on our porch.

This can only mean one thing— my barking made him drop it!

Next thing I know, the Big Brown Truck rattles away with a clang and a roar.

Whew! My job is done. "And don't ever come back!" I bark.

Hattie's clearly relieved the truck is gone. She grabs the box off the porch and whisks it inside.

Food Lady hurries over. She must not realize the danger is gone. "What is it?" she says to Hattie.

"Don't worry," I tell her. "I kept her safe as always." And now we have a box to play with!

Hattie says, "Fenway," in her sweetest voice.

We gather around the box. To my surprise, Hattie does not stop me from checking it out. I sink my teeth into the cardboard and rip away. Instead of scolding me, Food Lady laughs.

Hattie grabs one side; I grab the other. After more tugs and tears, the box rips open, revealing . . . a Frisbee!

5

THWOOP

I thrust my snout into the box. Whoopee! It smells like a Frisbee that no other dogs have played with. It must be my reward for scaring away that truck.

Hattie reaches into the box and pulls it out. "Ready, Fenway?" she says.

I back up. "I'm ready!" I bark. "I'm so ready!"

Hattie's elbow bends. She's going to fling the Frisbee!

I leap onto the couch, racing back and forth. Hooray! Hooray! I'm going to catch that Frisbee in midair!

"Hattie!" Food Lady snaps. She hurries down the hall to the back door and slides it open.

"Fenway, let's go!" Hattie says. I chase her outside to the Dog Park.

"Whoopee!" I bark, romping down the steps. "I'm finally going to do amazing tricks!" I head into the grass. I can hardly wait for Hattie to throw that Frisbee!

I watch her arm go back. She flicks her wrist, and the Frisbee goes flying.

WHIZZZZZ!

I run ahead of it. "I've got it! I've got it!" I bark.

The Frisbee is in the air for a long time. It's way higher than I can jump. But it's going to sink sometime, and when it does, I'll grab it!

My eyes are focusing on that Frisbee, but my ears are focusing on something else.

CHIPPER-CHATTER-SQUAWK!

I know that sound—a sneaky squirrel is coming into the Dog Park. I want to tell him to get out of here, but I'm busy watching the Frisbee. It's sailing . . . it's soaring . . .

CLATTER-CLATTER-CLATTER!

The squirrel is scampering along the top of the fence! I need to yell "Scram!" but the Frisbee is flying and flying—wait a minute! Is it starting to sink?

I watch the Frisbee. I open my jaws. I spring up. I'm about to chomp it when—

THWOOP.

The Frisbee lands ever so softly
in the grass ahead of me. Hey, that
wasn't supposed to happen!

I fall back down. It's that sneaky
squirrel's fault! I would've nabbed

the Frisbee in midair like Carmen if that guy hadn't shown up.

I'll get it next time. I chomp the hard plastic. While I'm bringing the Frisbee back to Hattie, I notice the middle is soft with swirly designs. But it's a Frisbee, and it's mine, and that's all that matters.

I drop it at Hattie's feet.

"Ready, Fenway?" She throws it again.

"Ready!" I race into the grass. Nothing will get in my way this time!

WHIZZZZZ! The Frisbee sails through the air.

I'm watching ... I'm watching ... I sprint toward the back of the Dog Park. "I've got it! I've got it!" I bark.

The Frisbee flies way up high. **WHIZZZZZ!**

CHIPPER-CHATTER-SQUAWK!

The Frisbee is spinning. It's soaring higher ... **WHIZZZZZ!**

I want to bark. I want to look at the fence. But I have to get that Frisbee . . . I want it so bad . . .

CHIPPER-CHATTER-SQUAWK!

The Frisbee begins to drop. I leap as high as I can. My jaws are snapping, and—

THWOOP. It lands gently in the grass. Again.

6

THE WALK

After lunch, Hattie clips on my leash and we head out the front door. Normally, I'd be excited about a walk, but right now I can't stop thinking about the Frisbee. That squirrel was the reason I couldn't catch it. If only I could play Frisbee someplace without squirrels . . .

I barely notice when Hattie strolls up the driveway next door. When the front door opens, our friend Angel appears. She smells like bubble gum and dirt.

Angel dashes away, and I hear the sound of jingling dog tags. She returns with Goldie and Patches on leashes. Hooray! Hooray! My friends are coming on a walk with us!

"Guess what, ladies?" I say as we head toward the street. The short humans stop while we sniff our favorite tree.

"You saved Hattie from another

squirrel?" Goldie says when we're finished sniffing.

Patches nudges her with her snout. "What, Fenway?" she asks.

I puff up my chest. "I got a Frisbee!"

"That's great news," Patches says. She snaps at a fly.

"Wow." Goldie looks surprised. "So now you're doing Frisbee tricks like that dog at the park?"

"Not yet," I say. "But I will. Very soon!"

The ladies exchange glances. We pass two more driveways and two more grassy spots, and then

Patches says, "You really don't need to do tricks to be amazing, Fenway."

"You're one of a kind," Goldie says.

I turn toward them. "You didn't see that dog Carmen," I say. "You didn't hear the clapping and cheering."

Patches snaps at the fly again.

Goldie watches a boy ride by on a bicycle.

My friends don't understand. As we near a row of bushes, I look away and start to wonder if—hey! That smell! The low branch is rustling. And is that a fluffy tail?

I dive in. "Go away, you sneaky
squirrel!" I bark.

The leash holds me back.
"Fenway," Hattie calls. Clearly, she
wants to keep walking.

She has the worst timing. "I'm
busy, Hattie!" I bark, trying to
lunge after that rodent.

CHIPPER-CHATTER-SQUAWK!

The squirrel takes off.

I back out of the bush and gaze up. I spot him tearing through the grass toward a pine tree.

"See, Fenway?" Patches says. "You sure have a lot of energy."

"And you're full of excitement," Goldie says.

I scowl at the ladies. Those are not tricks. Nobody claps for those things. Nobody cheers.

7

TOO MUCH WAGGLE?

When we're back home, Hattie flops on the couch with her notebook. She pats the cushion beside her. "Here, Fenway," she sings.

That means she wants to snuggle. And normally I would, too. But right now I have a better idea.

I give the Frisbee a chomp and rush over to the couch. I lay my head on Hattie's lap. I nudge the notebook with the Frisbee. She will see that I want her to throw it in here, where there are no squirrels.

"Aw, Fenway," she says with a giggle. She draws some more on the page, then gives me a gentle push.

But I can tell she doesn't really mean it. My tail swaying with excitement, I prance back and forth across the Lounging Place. Every time I pass Hattie, I give the Frisbee an extra waggle in case she's forgotten about it.

I drop down to think, and the Frisbee slides under the low table. All I have to do is get someone to throw this Frisbee for me. Then everything will be perfect.

I'd easily leap up and catch it. I'd even spin around in midair like Carmen.

Food Lady comes down the stairs with a basket that smells like dirty clothes on her hip. I rush over. "Do you wanna play?" I bark. "Please? Please?"

She barely notices me. That's just as well. Food Lady is no fun when she's focused on dirty clothes. Still, I don't lose hope until she rounds the corner and disappears through the basement door.

I sprint back to Hattie. I grab the

Frisbee and thrust my head on the couch. I give the Frisbee another waggle.

Hattie glances up. A smile spreads on her face. But her gaze drops back to her notebook.

I have to keep trying. I push the Frisbee under her hand. I tilt my head and look up at her in the cute way that she likes. My tail swishes wildly. "Please?" I whimper.

"Aw, Fenway," she sings. Her eyes brighten. She closes the notebook and sets down her pencil.

Yippee! She's getting it!

I run in circles around the Lounging Place. She eases off the couch and tiptoes over to the basement door.

I charge up behind her. My head is cocked and listening, just like hers. After a moment or two, Hattie crouches down, her finger to her lips. "Shhh," she says.

Whoopee! I know what this means! I let the Frisbee fall at her feet. Then I race back down the hallway toward the Lounging Place. I'm so ready!

I turn just in time to see the Frisbee fling from Hattie's hand.

WHIZZZZZ! It flies down the hall.

"I've got it! I've got it!" I bark. I keep my gaze on the soaring Frisbee as I gallop into the Lounging Place. The Frisbee's path is curving . . . it's sinking lower . . . I spring up, my jaws snapping—

SMACK! The Frisbee hits a tall lamp and drops onto the couch. The lamp teeters, and—**THUD**—I collide

with the low table. Then—*THUD*—
I land on the floor! A vase wobbles,
then—*SPLASH!*

Water trickles onto my head and down my front legs.

I hear stomping and then the basement door slams.

8

THE MESS

Food Lady appears with lots of gasps and yelling. Why is she so mad? I'm the one who didn't get the Frisbee. Plus, my head is soaked! I hate being soaked!

I give myself a good shake. That heavy, wet feeling goes away. Ah, so much better.

Food Lady's arms are waving. She shouts even more. Whoa, the dirty clothes in that basket before must have really upset her.

Hattie darts around the Lounging Place, grabbing things as if she's in a big hurry. What's going on?

As I chase after Hattie, I notice the changes. A second ago, the room was neat and tidy like always. Now the lower part of the couch is streaked with wetness. The tall lamp is lying sideways across one of the cushions. The lampshade has a tear in it.

Hattie lifts the tall lamp off the couch and sets it back in its spot. She smooths the torn spot in the shade. "Sorry, sorry," she mumbles to Food Lady. She sounds upset. She must feel just as bad as I do that I didn't catch the Frisbee.

I hurry after her. "Let's try again!" I bark. "I know I'll get it next time." I'm running alongside the low table when the rug suddenly feels wet and spongy. One of my front legs buckles and my head bonks the vase—*ouch!* Next thing I know, it's spinning.

Flowers and water spew out of it, and—

"Fenway!" Hattie cries.

Why's she yelling at me? I'm the one who got bonked!

Food Lady takes the vase and flowers and heads into the Eating Place. She stopped yelling, but she still smells mad.

I can't help but wonder how this happened. All we did was play Frisbee in the house!

Hey, that reminds me . . . I rush back and forth over the soggy rug, searching. My nose tells me it's here someplace.

I spring onto the couch and rummage through the cushions. I bury my snout under a pillow. Where did it go?

I trot the length of the couch. I climb onto one arm and peer behind it. I have to find it!

I lean over the other arm, glancing around. I notice Hattie dabbing at the wet spots in the couch with her shirt . . . Aha!

I fly off the couch. The edge of the Frisbee is sticking out from under it. I open my jaws to give it a chomp when—uh-oh!

Food Lady's hand grabs it first.

And from the look on her face,
she does not want to play.

9

THE TALL HUMMING BOX

I'm not sure how this happened, but the Frisbee is now in the Eating Place, way up high. If I'm in just the right spot, I can see it peeking out on top of the tall humming box where the cold food is.

This is bad news. I'll never catch the Frisbee if I can't even reach it!

Every time Food Lady or Fetch Man comes into the Eating Place, I look up at the Frisbee. "Don't you see my Frisbee up there?" I bark. I jump and jump. I swipe my paw against the tall humming box.

But they don't get it. Don't they know I want it? I must be doing something wrong. If only I could figure out what it is.

Later, when the Eating Place smells like yummy pasta and meatballs, Hattie finally comes downstairs. It was almost as if she was being punished for some reason.

I plop onto my bum and gaze up at her. I make the face she can never resist. "Please grab the Frisbee, Hattie," I whine. "I can't reach it!"

Somehow, she does resist. She

trudges over and sits in her seat at the table, where Fetch Man and Food Lady are ready to dig in to that wonderful pasta. She does not even look at me.

I slink onto the floor and whimper.

The next morning, something wonderful happens! Fetch Man and Hattie head into the car. "Ready, Fenway?" Hattie calls.

I romp into the garage. "I'm so ready! I'm so ready!" As soon as I get into the back seat, my tail goes wild—I can smell the Frisbee in Hattie's backpack!

When our car stops in the crunchy gravel at the Big Park, me and Hattie spill out. Hattie is just as excited as I am. She knows I'm going to snatch that Frisbee right out of the air. I can hardly wait to hear her cheering for me!

We have the whole park to ourselves like last time. I look around for squirrels, but I don't see any. I don't smell any, either.

Hooray! Hooray!

Hattie unclips the leash, and I take off. The instant she flings that Frisbee, I'll already be halfway across the grass with a big head start.

WHIZZZZZ!

I hear it! I run faster! It's going high and far, and I'm going to get it!

THWOOP.

It lands just ahead of me. Not

again!

I pounce on the Frisbee, my jaws open wide. But instead of chomping

it, I grab it with both front paws and begin to bite. And chew. I'm so mad, I want to tear this Frisbee apart!

"Fenway!" Hattie calls. She sounds worried. She's coming this way.

I chew and chew. The soft middle of the Frisbee is ripping out. Patooey! Patooey! I'm so done with this Frisbee!

I wiggle and squirm and—uh-oh! My whole head is poking through the Frisbee. I try to back out. I pull and I tug, but I'm inside the Frisbee. And I'm stuck.

10

A PRETTY GREAT TRICK

I swipe at the Frisbee with one paw, then the other. I give it a shake. I try thrashing. I shake some more.

I spring up. I bend and curl. The worst part is the Frisbee smell reminding me that it's right under my nose. But no matter what I do, it won't come off.

I whip my head from side to side. I buck up and down. I run in circles. It's no use. The Frisbee is going to be around my neck forever!

At last, I drop onto my belly and whimper. This is not the way it was supposed to be. I wanted to catch the Frisbee, not get stuck in it!

"Get me out of here!" I yelp.

CHIPPER-CHATTER-SQUAWK! floats down from the trees. Those sneaky squirrels must be planning to race into the park and take over. They're probably glad that I'm stuck and not chasing them.

I wish I'd never gotten this Frisbee. I wish I could make it go away. I wish I could bury myself in the grass and hide forever.

Suddenly, the Big Park is noisy. When did more dogs and humans arrive?

I smell that Rottweiler, Carmen. She's headed this way.

I hear Hattie and Fetch Man. It sounds like they're . . . laughing?

CHIPPER-CHATTER-SQUAWK! Even the squirrels think my problem is funny.

They're all enjoying the show. Fetch Man and Hattie are clapping. "Ha, Fenway!" they cry.

"What a trick!" Carmen says. She sounds impressed.

Huh?

I raise my head. Fetch Man and Hattie are smiling.

Hattie crouches beside me. She rubs behind my ears. "Attaboy, Fenway!" she says. Fetch Man does, too.

Carmen's tall human, Felipe, comes striding over. "Wow! Cool!" he cries.

"There's no other dog like you!" Carmen sinks onto her front legs, her bum up high. "Can you teach me how to do that awesome trick?" she says.

Gosh, all I did was get my head stuck in a Frisbee.

It wasn't like I twisted and flipped and caught the Frisbee in midair like Carmen. And everybody in the park is gathered around me, amazed. They are cheering.

I guess what I did is kind of amazing.

I give Hattie's hand a little lick. "What can I say?" I bark. "It's a pretty great trick."

She pulls the Frisbee off my head. Ah! I give myself a well-earned shake. That's better!

For the rest of the morning,

Hattie throws the Frisbee. I race after it and wait for it to land in the grass. I push my head through the hole and carry it back to her. I trot through the park with my tail high. There really is no other dog like me.

When I reach Hattie, I bow, and she lifts the Frisbee off my head. She rubs me all over. "Attaboy, Fenway!" she says, clapping and cheering. Every single time.

ABOUT THE AUTHOR

VICTORIA J. COE's books for middle grade readers include the Global Read Aloud, Amazon Teacher's Pick, and One School, One Book favorite *Fenway and Hattie* as well as three Fenway and Hattie sequels. **Make Way for Fenway!** is her first chapter book series. Connect with her online at victoriajcoe.com and on Twitter and Instagram @victoriajcoe.

ABOUT THE ILLUSTRATOR

JOANNE LEW-VRIETHOFF's passion and love for storytelling is shown through her whimsical and heartfelt illustrations in picture and chapter books. Joanne also loves discovering the world with her family by traveling and collecting memories along the way, giving her more inspiration for her illustrations. Her favorite downtime activities are reading YA books recommended by her daughter, looking at TikTok videos of dogs and cats, and watching the Discovery Channel. Currently, Joanne divides her time between Amsterdam and Asia. Connect with her on Instagram @joannelewvriethoff.

LOOK FOR THE NEXT

MAKE WAY FOR FENWAY!

CHAPTER BOOK!

fenway
AND THE
LOUDMOUTH BIRD